CONTENTS

PUBLISHED BY PETER HADDOCK LIMITED, BRIDLINGTON, ENGLAND.
© FERN HOLLOW PRODUCTIONS LIMITED
PRINTED IN INDIA

Spring in Fern Hollow

In Fern Hollow, as in other places, Spring is a time of great activity; a time for gardening, for whitewashing and for Spring cleaning.

6

It is a restless time of year when no-one can
stand still for very long, but after chatting to
you for a minute or two they will mumble,
"I really must get that door painted," or
"Dear me, it's May already, and I haven't
planted my vegetables yet," and off they will
rush to get things done!

It was Easter time and
Monty was helping his
Father, Mr. Tuttleebee, to
repair the roof, while Spud
and Heather played with
their Easter eggs.

In the shop Mrs. Tuttleebee
was wrapping some Spring flowers
for Mr. Willowbank.
"They will be a nice surprise Easter
present for Mrs. Willowbank," said the
Hedgehog.

8

It was such a beautiful Spring day, and it seemed so stuffy inside the old school house that Miss Crisp decided to take her class out of doors.

The lesson was in arithmetic, which was usually rather boring (to everyone except Clarence Hoppit, who was clever at that sort of thing), but today, in the fresh air, arithmetic didn't seem too bad at all!

It was a fine day for the Spring Jumble Sale in the Vicarage gardens, and Parson Dimly, who was looking after the Lucky Dip, was pleased to see that lots of animals had turned up.

Mrs. Dimly took care of the refreshments, while Lupin had lots of fun on the Jumble Stall, which was filled with clothes the Fern Hollow animals had cleared out during their Spring cleaning.   13

Constable Hoppit was taking a walk with
his family on his day off work, when they
were caught in an April shower! Clarence
and Clarissa hurried along with their
Mother, while Constable Hoppit picked up
little Horace and raced on in front.

Then, under the shelter of the beech trees,
they all watched the rainbow while they got
their breath back, and waited for the rain
to stop.

15

In Boris Blink's Antiquarian Bookshop, Boris and his assistant Leapy were Spring cleaning, when professor Sigmund Swamp dropped in, looking for a book on Famous Toads.

"I think you will find one in that pile over there," said Boris.
"Dear me!" exclaimed the professor. "It would be like looking for a needle in a haystack. I think I'd better come back tomorrow when you've got the books back on the shelves again."

Mr. and Mrs. Rusty had taken their cubs, Dusty, Rufus and Redvers out to fly a kite in the March winds. Rufus held onto the line, while Redvers chased around trying to catch the kite's tail, but soon it was flying so far out of reach that it was almost touching the clouds.

18

Summer
in
Fern Hollow

Everyone in Fern Hollow looks forward to
the Summer, to the lovely days spent
picnicking by the River Ferny and to the
visits to the seaside.

On their long summer holidays from
school, the little animals go swimming and
fishing, or play hide and seek in Windy
Wood.

The bumble bees bumble around amongst the wild flowers, dragonflies zoom low over the river and no-one feels very much like work, though of course there is still plenty to be done!

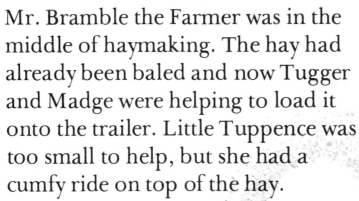

Mr. Bramble the Farmer was in the middle of haymaking. The hay had already been baled and now Tugger and Madge were helping to load it onto the trailer. Little Tuppence was too small to help, but she had a cumfy ride on top of the hay.

In the middle of the afternoon, Mrs. Bramble arrived with lots of lovely things to eat and drink. Then the busy badgers stopped work for a picnic.

Professor Sigmund Swamp was retired and spent most of his time picnicking by the River Ferny. He had travelled abroad and lived in the tropics, and was not at all worried by the hot weather. In fact, he was heard to remark that he thought the Summer had been rather cool!

Mr. Twinkle's family were spending a lovely Summer's afternoon by the pool in the garden. Mrs. Twinkle was relaxing under the shade of a mushroom, while Mr. Twinkle floated pleasantly around the pool on an airbed.

Sparky, Dash and Skipper played around on the springboard, and Midge practised her diving.

The Summer was so hot that the River Ferny had dried up, and there wasn't enough water to turn Mr. Croaker's mill wheel.

"Never mind," said Mrs. Croaker. "We can all take a holiday until the rain begins to fall again."
"Hooray!" cried Lily. "Can we go to the seaside?"
"Yes, of course," chuckled Mr. Croaker. "And Dipper can sail his yacht in the sea!"

At the Railway Station Mr. Twinkle was having trouble with some foreign visitors who had lost their tickets. Fortunately the problem was soon solved by old Stripey, the Porter, who found them lying on the platform.

30

Meanwhile Mr. Rusty, the Engine Driver, checked his wrist watch with Mr. Prickles' and blew the Bluebell's whistle to warn the passengers that it was time to leave.

31

At the Jolly Vole Hotel, Mrs. Crackleberry and Poppy were serving cold drinks and ice creams to the guests at the outside tables, when Jingle's taxi arrived with the foreign visitors. Mr. Crackleberry picked up the Raccoon family's luggage and led them off to their room. Unfortunately no one had remembered to pay Jingle!

Autumn
in
Fern Hollow

Autumn is a beautiful time of year in Fern Hollow. The trees of Windy Wood turn golden, red and orange, and there is a wonderful scent in the air.

Unfortunately, the fallen leaves do cause
the animals something of a problem,
because they all like to keep their gardens
tidy. Of course you can always make a little
bonfire of the leaves, but it is best to check
which way the wind is blowing first!

Mr. Prickles had taken a day off from his job as a guardsman at Fern Hollow railway station, to gather the fruit and nuts in Windy Wood. The expedition had been very successful and, with the help of Mrs. Prickles and Polly, Mr. Prickles had managed to fill his cart so well that there was hardly room for another acorn!

Jasper, Patch, Tugger and
Monty decided it would be
fun to raid an orchard.
Unfortunately for them
P.C. Hoppit came by on his
bicycle and caught them—all
except for Jasper the squirrel,
who was very quick at
climbing up and down trees,
and managed to run away.

Dilly and Pud's Hallowe'en costumes were the best in the village. This was hardly surprising as their parents, Mr. and Mrs. Thimble, were the Fern Hollow tailors.

Dilly and Pud's friends were dressed in pixie or goblin costumes and some of them wore masks so that you couldn't tell who they were!

41

In the heart of Windy Wood Mr. Chips and his sons Chucky and Flip were cutting down trees and chopping them up for firewood in preparation for the Winter.

The hard work had made them feel very hungry and they were all pleased when Mrs. Chips shouted that the soup was ready.

43

One gusty day in October Lord Trundle was taking a stroll around the grounds at Trundleberry Manor when he bumped into old Blodger, his gardener, who was having trouble with the fallen leaves. Every time Blodger swept them into a neat little pile, the wind came along and blew them away again!

45

Mrs. Bouncer poked the baked potatoes out of the bonfire and handed them round to the children.
"One for Patch, one for Pippa and one for little Toby," she said. "Be careful, they are rather hot."

Mr. Bouncer lit a sky rocket and it flew high up into the night sky.
"Good gracious," laughed Grandpa Bobber. "It looks like it's going all the way to the moon!"

Winter
in
Fern Hollow

Winter in Fern Hollow is more often than not very cold with plenty of snow. This suits some of the little animals very well. They can build snowmen, sledge and skate on the River Ferny.

But not everyone likes that sort of thing,
and some say that there is nothing
better than gathering a great big stack
of wood, making a nice warm fire and
maybe toasting a few crumpets.

49

Mr. Willowbank was a marvellous cobbler and could usually mend an old shoe so that you wouldn't have known it from a new one. But when Spike brought him Mr. Bouncer's Fireman's boots, he shook his head and said they would have to be thrown away.

"How on earth did your boots get such enormous holes in them?" asked Mrs. Willowbank.
"I put them by the fireside to dry," admitted Mr. Bouncer, "and they burnt."
"That was a silly thing for a Fireman to do," laughed Spike.

Jasper and Podger bustled excitedly into Brock Gruffy's shop. They had just emptied their Piggy banks and found that they might possibly have enough money to buy a sledge. Mr. Gruffy was very helpful and managed to find a super sledge at about the right price. Actually, it cost a bit more than the two little squirrels had managed to save, but the kind old Badger said that, seeing as it was them, they could have it anyway!

Mrs. Periwinkle could hardly believe
her eyes; Mr. Periwinkle had forgotten
to buckle up his postbag and all the
Trundleberry Manor Christmas Party
invitations were blowing away.

Fortunately Wally managed to catch up
with the bicycle and Mr. Periwinkle
came back to gather up the invitations.
"I hope I haven't lost any of them," he
worried.
"No one wants to be left out of the
Party I'm sure!"

54

Fergus was all tucked up in bed suffering from a terrible cold.

"Not to worry," said his Father, Dr. Bushy.

"We'll give you some medicine and you'll be right as rain in no time."

56

"Yes, we must get you well quickly Fergus," said
Mrs. Bushy, "The Trundleberry Manor Party is only a
few days away!"

In the bakery Mr. Acorn was busy baking lots of delicious things to eat for the Christmas party. Jiggy watched her Mother icing a cake, while Jasper did his best to help by fetching and carrying. As for little Podger, it was long past his bedtime and he had fallen asleep on the floor!

And then at last it was Christmas Day, and time for the Trundleberry Manor Christmas Party! Everyone turned up (obviously Mr. Periwinkle, the Postman, hadn't managed to lose any of the invitations), and they all agreed that it was the best Christmas party there ever was!

SIGMUND'S BIRTHDAY SURPRISE

The birds were singing and the early morning sunshine was glinting through the trees, as Mr Periwinkle the Postman came driving along the lane in his post van. Normally Mr Periwinkle did his rounds on his bicycle, but this morning he had an especially large birthday present to deliver to Sigmund Swamp. It was a long wooden crate, and rather strange snorting noises were coming out of it! The crate was very heavy and Sigmund had to help Mr Periwinkle to carry it into the house. "It says, 'From Uncle Oscar to Sigmund on his birthday' ", said Sigmund, reading the label. "I wonder what it can be."

Carefully, Sigmund began to prise the lid off the crate. As he did this the snorting noises from inside grew louder and louder, until at last the lid popped open and out crawled an enormous crocodile! In the twinkling of an eye, Mr Periwinkle rushed out to his van and drove away, and Sigmund scrambled up on top of a cupboard. Meanwhile, the crocodile began to gobble up the poor toad's breakfast. He was very hungry. In fact, he hadn't had a bite to eat since he left the Amazon jungle, where Uncle Oscar had caught him!

Having polished off Sigmund's breakfast, the crocodile still felt hungry and went off looking for more. He made his way through the garden and slid into the river Ferny. As he swam past the school, the children were playing football. Spike Willowbank gave the ball an extra hard kick which sent it flying over the playground wall. It would have landed in the river, but the crocodile caught it in his mouth and made a nice little snack of it.

"Good gracious," cried Mrs Prickles, almost jumping out of her shoes. "It's a crocodile!" And she scurried into her house and bolted the door behind her. As for the crocodile, he took a fancy to the washing and ate the lot, sheets, pillowcases and all.

Mrs Prickles's washing had been very tasty, but now the
crocodile sniffed the air and caught a scent that was
absolutely delicious. It was coming from the bakery where
Mr Acorn had just finished baking a batch of cream buns

and jam tarts. What a feast they made! The crocodile ate every last one of them, smacked his lips, and then devoured a shelf of crusty loaves.

"Go away at once," shouted Mr Acorn, waving his rolling pin angrily. But the greedy animal didn't leave until he had eaten everything in sight.

By this time, Sigmund had informed P C Hoppit about the escaped crocodile, and together they set out to track him down. They hadn't been searching long when Sigmund heard an odd little sound coming from behind a tree.
"Boo-hoo. Boo-hoo-oo."
It was the crocodile and he was crying.
"Dear me," whispered P C Hoppit. "What can be the matter with him?"
"I expect he's feeling lonely," replied Sigmund. "After all, he is the only crocodile in Fern Hollow."

"Yes," agreed P C Hoppit. "I think I'd better telephone Poppletown Zoo to come and take him away. There are bound to be other crocodiles at the zoo to keep him company."

Before long, a Zookeeper arrived in a large van with a
cage on the back. On the Zookeeper's instructions the
cage was baited with a tray of hot swiss rolls, supplied by
Mr Acorn. Then everyone hid themselves and waited.
The crocodile was still crying behind his tree, but when he

caught the delicious smell of the swiss rolls he quickly
perked up and crawled out to investigate. The moment he
was in the cage the Zookeeper leapt out from his hiding
place and locked the door.

"Hooray!" cried everyone.

"Mmmm," said the crocodile, munching the swiss rolls.

It turned out that Sigmund's Uncle Oscar had intended to send the crocodile to the zoo in any case, instead of which he had sent them a crate of Amazon honey, which was really Sigmund's birthday present. He had simply mixed up the labels. The crocodile settled in nicely at the zoo, where Sigmund visited him from time to time and fed him a few of Mr Acorn's cream buns!

PARSON DIMLY'S TREASURE HUNT

It was Sunday and Parson Dimly was busy in the church laying out the hymn books for the morning service. As he bustled around he sang to himself, "all things bright and beautiful." Suddenly another voice joined in.

"Chirp, chirp, chirp." The old mole looked up and saw a little sparrow. It had flown in through a large hole in the church roof.

"Good gracious," the parson exclaimed. "That hole must have been caused by the storm we had last night. I must get it fixed at once, but how on earth can I raise the funds?"

After giving the matter some thought, Parson Dimly decided to raise the money to mend the roof by holding a treasure hunt. The Fern Hollow animals all bought tickets and turned up with all kinds of vehicles. There were cars, motorcycles, a tandem, the fire engine and Sigmund Swamp on his penny farthing. In fact, the only animal who arrived on foot was Polly Prickles. Poor Polly — no-one thought she stood the slightest chance of winning the race to the treasure.

Now it was time to begin the treasure hunt by reading the first clue.

    "Look in a tree, in a little round hole
      which stands in a place by a happy old vole,"
read Parson Dimly.

Brock Gruffy realised at once what the clue referred to and quickly drove off to the Jolly Vole Hotel, where he jumped

out of his car and ran down to the river bank to the hollow
tree. Unfortunately poor Brock forgot to put the car's
handbrake on and his car rolled down the bank after him,
and with a great splash, ended up in the river!

83

The next animal to arrive at the hollow tree was Sigmund Swamp. Sigmund read the clue —

Now you're wondering what to do
Where the river is crossed you'll find the next clue.

"That must mean Ferny Bank Ferry," said the clever toad to himself. and away he went, pedalling furiously.

When Sigmund reached the ferry he rode out onto the jetty
to the signpost where he could see a piece of paper had been
pinned. Suddenly there was a loud bang and Sigmund fell off
his penny farthing. The poor toad had ridden over a nail and
punctured a tyre. 85

The clue pinned to the signpost at the Ferry read —
    The third clue you will find today
    Is where the farmer stores his hay.
It was easy to guess that this must mean Farmer Bramble's barn, and very soon the farm yard and the barn were crammed with traffic. Everyone had read the clue which was pinned to the barn door, but they had got themselves into such a jam that no-one could get out!

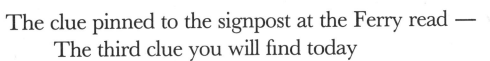

87

Eventually Polly Prickles arrived
at the barn. She was feeling
rather tired because of course she
had had to run all the way —
"To find the treasure run as fast
as you can
Back to the place where the hunt
began,"
puffed Polly, reading the clue on
the barn door. Then away
she ran as fast as she could back
to the vicarage garden.

In the garden Polly found a huge hamper of food and a trophy with "Winner of the Grand Treasure Hunt" inscribed on it. Perhaps this wasn't real treasure, but it had all been great fun and Polly decided to share the hamper with all the other contestants and Parson Dimly, so they all had a lovely picnic.

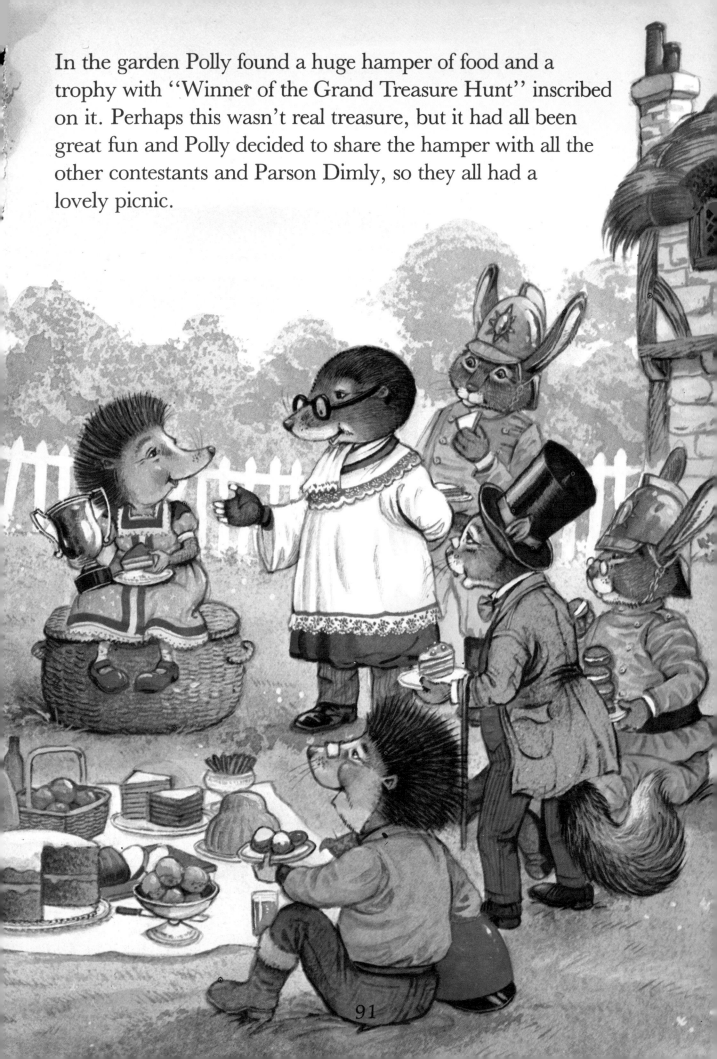

The next day Parson Dimly counted the money which the treasure hunt had raised, and was pleased to find that it easily covered the cost of mending the church roof. Naturally, the work was done by Mr Chips and his sons, Chucky and Flip, who made a very good job of it.

Fern Hollow

MR. CHIPS'S HOUSE

MR. WILLOWBANK'S
COBBLERS SHOP

MR. CROAKER'S WATERMILL

STRIPEY'S HOUSE

SCHOOL

THE JOLLY VOLE
HOTEL

RIVER FERNY

MR. ACORN'S
BAKERY

MR. RUSTY'S HOUSE

MR. PRICKLES'S HOUSE

POST OFFICE

BORIS BLINKS'S
BOOKSHOP

MR. TWINKLE'S
HOUSE

MR. TUTTLEEBEE'S
SHOP

MR. THIMBLE'S
TAILORS SHOP

WINDYWOOD